HORSE DIARIES
·Calvino·

HORSE DIARIES

Calvino

WHITNEY SANDERSON

illustrated by RUTH SANDERSON

RANDOM HOUSE NEW YORK

Text copyright © 2017 by Whitney Robinson
Cover art and interior illustrations copyright © 2017 by Ruth Sanderson
Photograph copyright © by Makarova Viktoria/Shutterstock (p. 145)

All rights reserved. Published in the United States by Random House
Children's Books, a division of Penguin Random House LLC, New York.

Random House and the colophon are registered trademarks of
Penguin Random House LLC.

Visit us on the Web! randomhousekids.com

Educators and librarians, for a variety of teaching tools, visit us at
RHTeachersLibrarians.com

Library of Congress Cataloging-in-Publication Data
Names: Sanderson, Whitney, author. | Sanderson, Ruth, illustrator.
Title: Calvino / Whitney Sanderson ; illustrated by Ruth Sanderson.
Description: New York : Random House, [2017] | Series: Horse diaries ; #14 |
Summary: In 1570s Spain, Calvino, an Andalusian horse, is purchased from the
Moreno estate in Seville to join King Philip's stable in Cordoba. | Description based
on print version record and CIP data provided by publisher; resource not viewed.
Identifiers: LCCN 2015039786 (print) | LCCN 2016019876 (ebook) |
ISBN 978-1-101-93779-2 (trade paperback) |
ISBN 978-1-101-93780-8 (hardcover library binding) | ISBN 978-1-101-93781-5 (ebook)
Subjects: LCSH: Andalusian horse—Juvenile fiction. | CYAC: Andalusian horse—
Fiction. | Horses—Fiction. | Spain—History—16th century—Fiction.
Classification: LCC PZ10.3.S217 Cal 2017 (print) | LCC PZ10.3.S217 (ebook) |
DDC [Fic]—dc23

Printed in the United States of America
10 9 8 7 6 5 4 3 2 1
First Edition

In memory of Thor, my golden sun horse

—W.S.

For Whitney

—R.S.

CONTENTS

"Oh! if people knew what a comfort to horses a light hand is . . ."
—from *Black Beauty*, by Anna Sewell

HORSE DIARIES
· Calvino ·

1

Southern Spain, 1570s

When I was a foal, the bulls were only dim black shapes moving across the horizon. Sometimes the ground trembled under my hooves from their distant stampedes. Sometimes my nostrils caught a whiff of their earthy scent. But they were as far away as the steppes blooming with wild flowers or the mountains rising blue and hazy beyond the neatly kept orchards and whitewashed stone buildings of the Moreno estate.

By late spring, the bulls were driven to their summer pastures in the mountains, and I forgot them. There was so much to explore in the vineyards, fields, and orchards surrounding the manor house and its stone stable.

Rasula and I could wander freely, for there were no fences. On our flanks we bore the brand of the Moreno estate, shaped like the curb bit that was still unknown to me. No thief could pass unnoticed through these provinces, where only a few landowners lived within a day's journey of each other, and every man knew his neighbors' brands as well as his own.

My dam was a favored pet of the family, Master

Moreno's wedding gift to his wife, Ana Sofia. With her lacy dappled coat and silken mane flowing nearly to the ground, Rasula charmed all who met her. The master often spoke of his *dos bellas damas*, or two beautiful ladies.

My sire, for whom I was named, was the master's own mount. He was like a great thundercloud on the horizon, sweeping closer only when the master came home from working beside his vaqueros in the mountains. His hooves seemed to shake the very leaves of the fruit trees that were the Moreno family's silver. The bulls, with their sleek coal-colored coats, were their black gold—more famous even than the estate's wine and oranges.

When the master returned, he would lean down and sweep his elder son, Joaquin, into the

saddle before him and hand him the reins so he
could play at being a real vaquero. Rico, the shy
younger brother, clung to Ana Sofía's skirts and
hid his face when the master called to him in his
booming voice.

There was always a fiesta in celebration of the master's return, with a roaring bonfire and people dancing and drinking sherry late into the night. It was also a time for the men to show off their favorite horses. In Andalusia, a vaquero's stallion was prized above all else he possessed.

The men rode across planks of wood to show off their mounts' high, prancing steps. The horses' necks arched against their bits, nearly touching their powerful chests. Everyone laughed when I strutted in among them and took my own turn clattering over the boards.

In the afternoons, Ana Sofia and her friends sat on the shaded portico, sipping cups of thick chocolate and waving their fans to stir the humid air. I often scrambled up the slippery stone steps to receive my share of treats and attention. When

Ana Sofia laughed, it sounded like the jingle of the silver bells she had sewn onto her fan.

The ladies called me *una pepita dulce*—a sweet nugget—and fed me strawberries. I was as much a pet as the nightingale that Ana Sofia kept in a golden cage on the porch. I often heard the bird's lovely, sad song floating across the yard at night.

Those were golden afternoons, but often restlessness struck like a spark inside me. Once I strayed too far from my dam's dappled warmth and found myself lost in the orchard at dusk.

The mist had settled so thickly that I did not know from which direction I had come. Ana Sofia's chickens had stopped their clucking, and the coo of the doves that roosted in the trees had ceased. A pungent, oily smell filled my nostrils, overpowering the delicate sweetness of the orange blossoms.

I was not afraid, because I'd never had anything to fear.

The mist swirled away to reveal a strange animal crouched between the trees. It had a snub-nosed face and eyes that glowed like embers. Its tufted ears and thick tail were tipped with black, as if they'd been singed with soot. Clenched in its jaws was the limp body of Ana Sofia's favorite speckled hen.

I felt torn between two instincts: one to charge the animal, and the other to flee. It was normally the watchdog Oro's job to protect the hens. But he was not in sight, so I had to defend the Moreno flock.

I reared up on my hind legs to make myself

appear larger than I was. The animal dropped the hen and slashed the air with claws like giant thorns. I struck out with one foreleg, then the other, my small, sharp hooves flashing high.

The animal turned and bolted into the mist. I reared again and kicked out my hind legs in triumph. My first foe vanquished!

Calvino? I heard my dam's distant call.

Here I am! I bellowed back, and waited for her to find me. With her dapple-gray fur, she appeared as if the mist itself were taking shape.

There was an animal! I cried, cantering in circles around her. *It was big like Oro, and covered in stripes. It had one of the chickens in its teeth, but I chased it away. Now the chicken has gone to sleep.*

Rasula lowered her head to sniff the hen, which was lying motionless in the grass.

It is not asleep, she said. *The animal you saw was a lynx, and it has killed Ana Sofia's good hen. It has been a long time since I have seen a lynx—they usually stay in the mountains. I will tell Oro to keep a closer watch.*

I can guard as well as any dog, I said, puffing out my chest with pride.

Yes, you were very brave, said my dam, rumbling with amusement.

Tired from my adventure, I flopped down in the grass. The mist had cleared and the moon cast its peaceful light over the hacienda. The hens began to cluck again, Oro darted like a watchful shadow around the edges of the orchard, and order was restored to my small world.

2

Master Moreno

Golden dust filled my eyes and nose and settled on my sweating back. Ahead of me, Rasula's hindquarters swayed as she trotted through the wheat. With each circle around the field, she trampled the cut stalks and separated them from the ripe heads of grain.

My own small hooves barely made a dent in the straw. It tangled around my legs and threatened to send me sprawling.

Remember, a proud step makes for light work. My dam's sweet neigh floated back to me through the haze.

Rasula never seemed to trip or tire. Her ears swiveled back to listen to young Joaquin, who stood in the center of the field holding a braided leather whip. Were it not for this instrument, and the sting I knew it contained, my legs would wander where they pleased instead of wading through this sea of prickly stalks.

But what if it were possible to separate the whip from the boy? My trot slowed as my mind raced, and the whip flicked across my hindquarters.

Instead of quickening my pace, I whirled

to face the boy and charged at him with flattened ears. Joaquin let out a shout of surprise and dropped the whip. He made a dash for the field's edge and found refuge in the branches of an orange tree.

Rasula whinnied anxiously from the field, but

I paid no heed. I galloped and bucked in triumph around the tree where I had trapped my quarry.

An unripe orange hit me on the head. Another struck my rump. I skittered to a halt and turned to face my adversary with new respect.

One of the hired hands, Fausto, walked by on

his way to tend the orchard. "What are you doing in that tree, young Master Joaquin?" he inquired.

"He charged me!" cried the boy, pointing to where I stood—just outside the range of flying oranges.

Fausto looked at me doubtfully. "That's just a foal, son, not a fighting bull."

Joaquin kicked the tree trunk with the heel of his boots. "I don't see why I have to work in the fields, anyway," he muttered. "I want to ride out to the cattle with Papá."

The worker's sun-browned face crinkled with laughter. "If you can't manage an unruly colt, you wouldn't last long in a herd of wild cattle. I guess your father will take you out to the steppes when he thinks you are old enough to handle a *garrocha* pole."

The boy tossed a green orange sulkily from hand to hand. Fausto gave me a friendly slap on the rump and continued on his way.

Joaquin climbed down from the tree, eyeing me warily. I was a naughty colt, but not a vicious one, and my point had been made. I trotted back to the wheat field with a light step, ready to work again—but now there could be no doubt that it was my generosity of spirit, and not fear of punishment, that kept me trotting in circles around the boy and his whip.

My dam scolded me with a sharp nip on the crest of my neck. Poor Rasula. I had inherited the dapples of her coat, but not the goodness of her nature.

Joaquin had taken up his whip and was striding toward me with a dangerous glint in his eyes.

However, his vengeance was interrupted by the sight of a horse and rider galloping across the broad stretch of grassland between the estate and the mountains.

I recognized Tito, the master's most trusted vaquero, and his stallion, Amadeo. The pair drew to a halt when they reached the edge of the wheat field, and Tito dismounted.

"Where is your mother?" he asked Joaquin, his voice grave. Amadeo's ribs were heaving, and lines of sweat ran down his roan coat.

"In the house, preparing for the fiesta," Joaquin replied. "Papá promised I could go with him to the horse fair this year. But Rico has to stay home with Mamá," he added smugly.

The vaquero said nothing, only rested his hand briefly on the boy's shoulder, then hurried toward the house. Joaquin trotted at Tito's heels, peppering him with questions.

Amadeo stood where Tito had left him, catching his breath. I noticed a dark red blossom staining his chest.

Amadeo, you've been gored! said my dam, tossing her head with concern.

Only grazed, replied the stallion, shifting uncomfortably from hoof to hoof. *There was a stampede at the mountain pass. One of the bulls turned on us. I'm afraid . . . Calvino and the master were killed, Rasula.*

No! That cannot be. My dam backed up a few steps, shaking her head. Then she spun on her haunches and galloped away into the orchard.

I trailed after her but stopped at the edge of the field and let out an anxious whinny. From deep in the orange grove, I heard my dam's ringing reply. But I knew she was not calling for me.

I remembered the magnificent pale gray stallion and the man sitting so tall and proud on his back. Could they really be still and lifeless now, like the chicken crushed in the jaws of the lynx?

From the corner of my eye, I saw a figure emerge from the house. It was Joaquin. He ran across the carefully kept lawn to the tangled meadow beyond. He fell to his knees and began ripping the wild flowers from the ground— delicate blooms of lavender, tough yellow gorse, spiny prickly pear—and flung them in all directions. Then he sat crouched in the grass like a wild animal, not making a sound.

A soft cry made my ears flicker back. Little Rico was clinging to a stone pillar of the portico.

He called his brother's name but did not leave the shelter of the house. He clutched at the climbing ivy as if he feared the wind might carry him off if he let go.

It was strange—I hardly knew the master, or my own sire. They spent most of their time tending the cattle in the mountains or traveling to distant cities. But somehow their presence had remained at the hacienda, creating a sense of safety and abundance.

Now that feeling was gone. The whitewashed manor house looked small against the looming mountains. The grapes and oranges seemed to wilt on their stems.

Tito and the other vaqueros brought the master's body home for burial. My sire had been laid to rest on the open steppes. Rasula pulled the cart with the master's coffin to the church in Seville. I was tied up inside the stone stable so I would not follow her.

When the family returned from the funeral, Joaquin broke away and ran into the barn. He sat in the straw beside me, his head buried in his arms. I reached out my nose to touch his dark hair.

A shadow fell across the doorway. It was Tito, holding a pair of spurs with a star-shaped rowel. Joaquin stood up quickly, swiping at his tear-streaked face.

Tito handed the spurs to Joaquin. "These belonged to your father," he said. "Now they are yours." The boy slowly fastened the leather straps over his boots. Then he stood up straight, his chin jutting now instead of quivering.

"Go inside to your mother," said Tito. "She needs both of her sons with her."

The heavy spurs, too wide for Joaquin's boots, dragged on the ground and left their impression in the dirt. They were a man's spurs, but there was no time for the young Master Moreno to grow into them.

3

Doma Vaquera

The visitors who came to see Ana Sofia now were dressed in black. There were no bonfires, no music, no hot chocolate and gossip on the porch. There was no more of Ana Sofia's silver-bell laughter.

In the fall, Rasula was shut into the stable so

I could be weaned from her. She called for me, but I had taken my nourishment from grass instead of milk for months. It was little Rico who stole outside at night to calm her quivering neighs.

Joaquin had grown into an angry, flint-eyed boy since his father's death. He did a man's work on the estate, picking oranges and stacking straw alongside the hired hands. But sometimes, when no one was looking, I saw him throw rocks to knock the doves' nests out of the trees.

In December, the ground frosted over and the whole world sparkled. The next day a multitude of dots appeared like grains of black pepper spilling down the mountain slopes. As they grew nearer, they became a churning sea of cattle. Men on horseback galloped alongside them.

The vibration of their hooves on the ground

stirred something in my blood. Before I knew it, I was racing out to meet the herd. A huge black bull ran at the front. His neck and chest were so heavy with muscle that his hindquarters seemed to belong to a different animal.

He spotted me, let out a bellow, and swung away from the pack, bearing down on me with breathtaking speed.

I ducked to the side by instinct rather than thought. The bull's horns caught in my tail,

jerking a few strands loose. Then the rest of the herd overtook us, and the bull galloped on, snorting and shaking his massive head.

My heart raced and my legs felt as jiggly as marmalade. And I wanted to do it again!

Be careful that your pretty coat is not marred by scars, little desbocado, called one of the ranch horses. *Have you not heard that caution is the greater part of wisdom?* He was a *hacas*, a part-bred, with his mane and tail cut short instead of

left long and flowing like a pure Spanish horse's.

Desbocado—runaway—I liked the sound of that. But I heeded the message and fell back to frolic among the yearling calves. They were safer adversaries, with only nubs for horns.

I touched noses with the shy, half-wild mares who kept the vaqueros supplied with foals to train and sell. The master had handpicked Rasula from this herd when she was just a filly, beguiled by her unusual beauty.

All that winter and the following spring, I roamed with the cattle and horses on the open range between the estate and the mountains. Rasula was happy to spend her life grazing like a living sculpture on the hacienda lawn, and I had also been content to be petted and admired.

But now that I had found my place among the

cattle, I felt joy unfurling like a flag inside me. *This* was where I belonged and where I stayed for two full cycles of the seasons.

When the herd returned to the mountains in the spring of my third year, I went with them. So did Joaquin, now fourteen years old. The boy had taken to riding Amadeo—the roan stallion, long since healed from his injury, made up for what Joaquin lacked in experience and caution. Like every good ranch horse, he was trained in the *doma vaquera* style, so that his rider needed only the lightest touch of one hand on the reins to guide him. Above all, he kept his own eyes and ears alert for what the vaqueros might miss.

Caution was a lesson that no one escaped, living among the cattle. The cows and calves were unpredictable—peaceful at times, irritable at others. But the bulls were always dangerous. One toss of their great horned heads could put a mortal wound in the belly of a horse or a man.

The vaqueros guided the movements of the cattle with long wooden *garrocha* poles. Sometimes they seemed like frail tools, as if the men were trying to guide an avalanche with river reeds.

At the end of the day, both the vaqueros and their stallions were bone-tired and covered in dust. One evening, Amadeo lingered close to the warming flames of the campfire instead of joining the herd to graze.

"What's the matter with him?" asked Joaquin, setting aside his meal of corn masa and beef jerky to check the stallion for injuries.

"Amadeo is only feeling his age," said Tito.

"He has been working the cattle since you were a baby riding a wooden hobbyhorse. Now he is having trouble keeping up with a young conquistador like you."

Tito left the campfire and walked over to where I grazed. "Maybe it's time you put a saddle on this colt of yours," he said, running his hand over my short, well-muscled back.

"Of mine?" Joaquin echoed, his brows unknitting from their usual glower.

"Your father would have made a gift of him when you were old enough," said Tito. "He would have helped you train him, too."

"I watched my father ride," Joaquin said quickly. "I was always watching him. I know how to break a colt."

Ever since the time I had chased him into the

orchard, I had never felt that Joaquin had much affection for me. But now he looked at me with new interest.

The next day, Joaquin lassoed me with his braided reata and took me back to the hacienda. I had grown used to my freedom, and I kicked up my heels in rebellion. But Amadeo cut off all my efforts at escape, and eventually I gave in and trotted willingly beside them.

As we neared the estate, I saw Rico oversee-ing the fall grape harvest, mounted on Rasula. My dam fluttered her nostrils in greeting, and I whinnied back to her.

"Still prancing around on that mare?" Joa-quin taunted his brother. "Help us drive the cattle sometime and you will see why men ride stallions."

After a year apart, the difference between

the brothers was striking. Joaquin strutted like a young bull, while Rico moved as cautiously as a wild deer.

Joaquin left me in the stable with Amadeo. Rico brought us each some water and a pail of corn. It was a rare treat after foraging for all our food in the mountains.

Master Joaquin may be growing in inches, but not in wisdom, remarked Amadeo, plunging his nose into the corn. The stallion's sides bore white marks where Joaquin's spurs had gouged away the fur. *He is like a colt who was weaned too soon and learned no gentleness of manner. I do not envy you, being broken by him.*

Iron on Iron

In the morning, Joaquin entered the stable with the bridle my sire had worn. He slipped it over my head before I could protest. The *bocado* bit was heavy in my mouth. The slightest pressure on the reins caused the metal *serreta* noseband to dig into the sensitive bones of my face.

Joaquin tied me to a ring on the wall and left me there for two nights. He gave me a little water, but I had no more food. My neck ached from the strain of being forced to hold my head so high. At first I was filled with rage and kicked out at the walls of my stall.

By the third day, I began to feel dizzy and weak. Joaquin released me into the circular pen the master had used for breaking horses. I galloped around the curved stone perimeter, seeking the security of a corner but finding none.

Whenever I tried to stop or change direction, the lash of Joaquin's whip—the same he had held when threshing the wheat—drove me forward again.

Anger overcame my weariness, and I turned and charged at Joaquin, this time not in the spirit of play.

But this time, Joaquin was armed with more than unripe oranges. His reata hissed through the air and caught me by the hind leg. A quick jerk, and I crashed to the ground.

I lay still while the world spun around me. How was it that Joaquin—the boy I had played games with, as if he were another foal—had turned on me like a mad watchdog savaging its own flock?

Joaquin leaned down and tied something to my ankles. I thrashed to my feet and found that my legs had been bound together with hobbles. *Traitor!* I thought, and my shock warmed into fury once more.

Joaquin grabbed the sheepskin saddle that had belonged to his father and flung it onto my back. He cinched the girth tight under my belly and swung up into the saddle. The hobbles would not allow me to bolt forward or back up.

But I could rear.

I flung my body high into the air. Joaquin shouted and jerked on the *serreta*. The pain only made me rise higher, higher, until my feet slipped in the dirt and I fell backward.

Joaquin rolled away before I hit the ground, but the saddle was crushed beneath me.

I tried to lift my head. A bolt of pain shot through my neck and back. Joaquin moved into my field of vision. He lowered his hand toward my bridle, as if to release the *serreta*.

No—it must be a trick! My teeth grazed his hand and I tasted blood. The boy's eyes blazed. He grabbed the whip from the dirt where it had fallen.

"*Joaquin!* Do not strike that horse again," a stern voice said from the edge of the corral.

It was Tito. He strode into the corral and took the whip from Joaquin. His strong, sure hands unfastened the hobbles from my legs. I scrambled to my feet and limped as far from my captors as the fence would allow.

"When you or your brother disobeyed your father, what did he do?" Tito asked Joaquin. His voice was calm, but anger was present in his stiffened shoulders and stern expression.

"Switched us with his belt," said the boy. "But only me. Rico was always good."

"And was it the sting of the lash that made you wish to undo your misdeeds?"

Joaquin was silent, staring at the ground. Then he shook his head.

"You cannot train a Spanish horse with iron on iron," said Tito. "Lesser men train lesser horses that way, but you will shatter that horse's spine before you break his will."

A cooling breeze found its way into the pen. I lifted my head to meet it. The *serreta* cut into my nose, and I squealed with pain. Joaquin looked at me as if he were seeing me for the first time.

"A stallion who obeys out of fear will flee instead of standing with his rider in the hour of truth," said Tito.

Joaquin's black eyes glittered with tears that would never fall. Tito took something from his pocket and handed it to Joaquin. It was a glass jar filled with amber liquid.

"In training a horse, there is a time for iron and a time for honey," he said. "Men like your father knew the difference."

Joaquin took the jar of honey and put it in the pocket of his calfskin vest. Slowly, he walked over to me and removed the crushed saddle from my back. I was too exhausted to challenge him. He slipped off my bridle. There was blood on my bit and in the teeth of the *serreta*.

Joaquin brought me food and water in the corral. Although a powerful thirst had built in me, I would not approach the brimming pail until he had left the corral.

Later, under a moon as round and bright as one of Ana Sofia's pearl earrings, the boy returned with the jar that Tito had given him. I bared my teeth in warning as he approached.

"*Calvino* . . ." Something in the way he spoke made my ears flicker forward. My nostrils caught a whiff of sweetness. He held no whip, and the spurs were gone from his boots.

I did not move away, but neither did I lower my head to meet his hands. I was a statue of cold marble in the moonlight.

Joaquin anointed the honey onto the bridge of my nose and the cracked corners of my mouth. I began to lick and chew despite myself. Joaquin rested his hand on my nose where it curved slightly, like a falcon's beak.

His touch reminded me of the *serreta*, and I flinched away. What reason had I to submit to the will of this boy, who demanded obedience without earning it?

I pushed my nose roughly against his chest and felt his heart beating like a startled rabbit's. With one toss of my head, I could have flung him high into the air.

Joaquin reached again into the glass jar and held up his palm. It would be easy to claim his fingers as well as the offering. But after a trembling moment, I plunged my nose into his hand and took only the honey.

Joaquin uncapped another jar that held a salve of fat and herbs. He rubbed it into the strained muscles of my neck and back. When I grew tired of his attention, I moved away and cantered in a circle around the corral, showing that neither my stride nor my spirit had been broken.

"You are the equal of your sire in every way," murmured Joaquin, watching me with his dark eyes. "I can only pray that someday the same will be true of myself."

Love is not earned with a few drops of honey.

But I was bred like Rasula, like my sire, like all Andalusian horses—with no place for fear in my heart when danger had passed.

By the time the light shining down on us had turned from night's silver to day's gold, the boy's hands had learned the power of a softer touch, and the jar of honey had been licked clean.

The Goodwill of Angels

Trust was built from need on the rugged steppes, and devotion followed. The vaquero and his horse depended on each other for survival. There were rivers to cross, rocky slopes that could shatter the legs of horses or cattle, and ravines filled with spiny broom and stinging nettle. Wolves stalked in the forest, and wild boar could be fiercer than the cattle.

Joaquin's manner was not always gentle, but he proved many times that he valued my life as equal to his own. Once, I startled a deadly asp viper that was sunning itself on a flat rock on the peninsula. Joaquin saw it before I did. He shouted and let go of the calf he was holding down to be branded. Without hesitation, he stepped between me and the snake and crushed it with the branding iron.

In time, I had a chance to repay his loyalty. When we were driving the cattle home from the mountains, a sideswipe from a bull's horns caught Joaquin's leg and swept him out of the saddle.

I turned my body sideways to shield him from

the oncoming herd. The cattle plunged around me. Their bodies fell heavily against mine, and their horns raked my sides. I knew that to move would mean the death of my rider. Joaquin was lucky to escape with a badly crushed hand and I with several deep gouges on my flanks.

When we reached the Moreno estate, Ana Sofia and Rico were waiting as they had once waited to greet Joaquin's father. Ana Sofia's face grew pale when she saw Joaquin's bandaged hand. "Mother of Mercy, Chimo," she said, using her pet name for her elder son.

"It's all right, Mamá," said Joaquin. "God has given us all more fingers than we need, has he not?"

Ana Sofia shook her head. "You are so much like your father, living on the goodwill of angels."

A look of pride crossed Joaquin's face until Rico said, "I guess Papá's goodwill ran out."

When they were younger, the two years between the brothers had not seemed like much. Now Rico looked like a weanling colt beside a fully grown stallion.

The boys struggled to run the hacienda, as the master had seemed to do so effortlessly. The family's silver trickled thin. Many of the vaqueros left to work on other estates or crossed the ocean to the promised riches of the New World.

It was a relief when April came, the month of spring grass and of the horse fair in Seville. Everyone was eager to see the city after a long, isolated winter on the hacienda. On the day of the fair, Rico hitched Amadeo to Ana Sofia's stylish two-wheeled cart. Rasula's new foal was too young to be separated from her, so she stayed behind.

Joaquin rode ahead with the vaqueros, guiding a group of a dozen newly branded weanlings and forty head of yearling cattle.

"Are you sure you don't want to ride Calvino and let me drive Mamá for once?" he said, circling back to taunt his brother. "The cattle are only babies—they won't hurt you."

It was late afternoon when we reached Seville. The narrow streets were packed with carriages, livestock, and running children. I helped to herd the cattle and the weanlings through the crowded square and into the temporary pens outside the city walls.

In a field nearby, a crowd had gathered for *acoso y derribo*—the trial of running young steers and knocking them down with *garrocha* poles to test their temperaments. It was also a way for the vaqueros to display their skill and, more importantly, their horses.

The men had traded their everyday clothes for their best: dark wool trousers, flared at the knee, and matching short jackets with colorful shirtwaists. On their heads, they wore felt hats fastened beneath their chins with silk straps.

The vaqueros jeered with laughter as a wiry steer leaped like a trout at the touch of the

garrocha pole. "You're supposed to roll him, Valdez, not scratch his back!"

Joaquin separated a big yearling from the Moreno herd and prodded him over to join the crowd. When our turn came, he set his steer loose in the grassy aisle formed between the rows of onlookers.

Joaquin held me back to give the calf a head start, then spurred me into a gallop. My heart leaped with the thrill of the chase, and in a dozen

ground-swallowing strides, I had closed the gap between us. Joaquin lowered his *garrocha* pole so it was level with the steer's hindquarters.

With one swift thrust, he sent the animal tumbling to the ground. The steer bellowed in surprise but quickly regained his footing and turned back on us, shaking his small—but still sharp—horns. Joaquin removed his sombrero and held it down so that the steer appeared to be wearing the hat as he circled us. Laughter rippled through the crowd.

But I noticed one person who was not laughing—a man dressed differently from the vaqueros, in a ruffled silk shirt, a short jacket elaborately embroidered with gold thread, and leather *polainas* over his boots that looked as fine and soft as the velvet of a black mare's nose. He gazed at me intently from the back of a handsome but rather fat bay stallion.

Joaquin set his spurs into my ribs and tightened the reins. I rose up into a rear and the crowd whistled and applauded. Joaquin tipped his sombrero to the audience and let the steer escape to join the other calves huddled at the far end of the field.

"Joaquin Moreno!" A young woman waved to us from the crowd, silver bracelets jingling on her arm.

"Buenos dias, Inez," said Joaquin, and I recognized the eldest daughter of our neighbor to the south. I had not seen her since the master's funeral. She was dressed much more festively today, in a ruffled red dress with a rose tucked behind her ear. "How are you? Has your father

brought many cattle to the fair?" he asked in an unusually pleasant tone.

"Not this year. He has leased the grazing rights to another fifty hectares of land from the Crown, so he is looking to buy instead of sell," said Inez. She took the flower from behind her ear and twirled it in her hand. "Is your mother well? How is her health?"

Joaquin and Inez exchanged more pleasantries. Then he reached down to offer her his arm. In a moment, she was sitting on my back, perched sideways behind my saddle.

We rode back into the city. Flowers were strewn across the ground, and their scent mingled with the rich smells of sherry and roasted meat. A band of Gypsy musicians began to strum their guitars and shake their castanets.

People clapped their hands and stomped their feet to keep time, and soon the square was whirling with dance. I was glad to see Ana Sofia among them, laughing as I had not seen her laugh in a long time.

I stepped gaily in time with the music while Joaquin promenaded around the city with Inez. The streetlamps glowed like fireflies on their iron posts, and many people were out strolling or driving in the fair spring evening.

I spotted Rico kicking a leather ball with some other boys in an alleyway.

"He is still just a child . . . ," murmured Joaquin, reining me to a halt while he watched his brother play.

We returned to the crowded square. Joaquin tied me to a hitching post and helped Inez down from my back. They danced the flamenco while I exchanged whinnies with a fetching mare with colorful silk ribbons braided into her long mane and tail, lamenting the distance between us.

That night, the Moreno family stayed at the home of friends in the city. I slept in the crowded cattle pen, guarded by several vaqueros who made pillows of their saddles. Fires from the Gypsy camps glowed in the distance.

The wail of their music went on late into the night and made my hooves want to keep dancing to its wild rhythm.

6

The Horse Master

By morning, the carnival atmosphere had been replaced by a businesslike air. Buyers moved purposefully from pen to pen, examining animals and writing up contracts of sale.

A rancher from the north bought two colts and twenty head of Moreno cattle. A spice merchant from the city chose a bright chestnut filly as a wedding present for his daughter. Near the end of the day, Inez's father stopped by and spoke for the rest of the cattle.

Joaquin and Rico prepared for the journey back to the estate while Ana Sofia sat on the high seat of the cart, counting pieces of silver from a velvet purse. Her brow was knotted with worry, and she turned the bag over again as if hoping more coins would fall into her palm.

Nearby, a shepherd boy released a seemingly endless stream of sheep from their pens. To my surprise, I noticed a man pushing his way through the flock—it was the rider of the bay stallion I had seen yesterday.

"*Buenos dias*," said the man as he reached our party. He was out of breath, and his elegant clothes were covered in curls of Merino wool. Ana Sofia and Rico echoed his greeting. Joaquin only grunted and swung the heavy ranch saddle onto my back.

"Your horse impressed me greatly during the *acoso y derribo* tournament," the man continued. "I have just been compensated for a large sum of silver that was stolen during my journey, and I am now at liberty to make an offer for him."

"He is not for sale," Joaquin said brusquely, and cinched the girth beneath my belly with a sharpness that made me bare my teeth.

"I am prepared to pay three thousand reales."

"Why, that is a king's ransom!" cried Ana Sofia, lifting the hem of her long skirt and stepping down from the cart.

"Then it is fortunate that I represent a king,

señora," the man replied. "Forgive me, for I have not introduced myself—I am Diego López de Haro, horse master to His Majesty King Philip the Second."

Ana Sofia seemed at a loss for words. Finally, she regained her composure and introduced herself and her sons. Rico's eyes were wide as he took in the man's ornate attire, more lavish than anything Master Moreno had owned. "Surely you could find more exotic and valuable animals here," said Ana Sofia. "A Barb from Africa, or a destrier with the strength of five ordinary horses."

"The king believes the horses bred in Andalusia to be without equal," replied the horse master, "and he wishes their reputation to spread throughout the world."

De Haro stepped forward and ran his fingers

through my mane, as if he were a silk weaver testing the quality of an expensive bolt of cloth. "He is sizable but not heavy," he said. "Even at rest he stands like he is on parade. His face could not be surpassed by any sculptor's chisel, and his dappled color is favored by the king."

Ana Sofia's fan fluttered like a moth's wings before her face. "Your price is generous," she replied, "but the stallion belongs to my son, and the decision must be his."

Joaquin did not answer while he put on my bridle. I flung my head high as I always did when I first felt the touch of the *serreta*. But once the headstall rested snugly and the fringed *mosquero* had been smoothed over my brow, I quickly settled.

"Calvino is a lion among horses," Joaquin finally said to de Haro. "But I am a better horseman now than when I trained him, as certain habits of his remind me. And three thousand reales will pay off the many debts that have accumulated since my father's death. If you believe you can master him, he is yours."

"Are you certain, Chimo?" asked Ana Sofia.

Joaquin nodded.

"Then I have but one further condition for you, Señor de Haro," she declared.

"Yes, señora?" asked the horse master, arching one eyebrow.

"Take my son as your student and apprentice," said Ana Sofia. "Teach him to ride as a gentleman rides and educate him. When he is grown, find a place for him in the court so that his future is secure."

De Haro looked at Joaquin with the same critical eye he had turned on me. "I have never accepted a pupil who was not born of the noble class," he said. "But I have seen him ride, and he is like a chunk of rough sapphire that could dazzle when properly cut. If he wishes to remain with his horse, I will accept him."

"No," said Ana Sofia, shaking her head so that her gold earrings clattered. "Not Joaquin— I want you to take Rico."

7

A Gilded Cage

The journey to Córdoba took four days. A dirt track, hardly visible in places, formed the only road through the plains that shimmered with a rainbow of spring flowers. As we traveled north, the path ascended into rocky foothills with groves of hardy cork and olive trees. My spirits were high, for I thrived on adventure, and I was delighted with these new sights and smells and tastes.

De Haro had bought twenty mares in Seville, and they traveled in a chain behind his huge mahogany carriage, each mare's tail knotted to the soft leather collar circling the neck of the horse behind her. Eighteen of the mares were gray, like me. All strung together, they were like a strand of pearls.

I had determined early in the course of our journey that I would not be ridden by the child. He was accustomed to riding gentle Rasula and was easily unseated. So I carried the horse master himself, and Rico rode de Haro's bay stallion, Campeón.

The horse master was a puzzle to me. His body

was still in the saddle, and his grip on the reins was featherlight. At first I thought I might rid myself of him quickly and travel as I pleased, perhaps in closer quarters to the mares.

But no matter how I spun and feinted, his balance was unchanged. It seemed that his hand could transform from silk to steel and back again in the span of a few moments, depending on whether my actions pleased him.

When I finally yielded to the bit, I was newly aware of the muscles in my arched neck and tucked hindquarters. It was as if the horse master's seat and hands had collected the power in my body so that no movement was wasted. The feeling was so new to me that I walked quietly, mouthing the bit, and set aside my interest in the mares for the time being.

Anyway, as long as I traveled with Campeón, I did not lack for conversation. The stallion had been born in the royal stables, and he told me about his life there from the moment of his foaling.

. . . So now, after four years of the most disciplined schooling, I have progressed to the alta escuela, *the highest level of* doma clásica *riding,* he said. *My specialty is the* piaffe *between the pillars, like so. . . .*

He demonstrated a mincing gait in which he set his hooves down in the precise spot from which he had lifted them.

You have spent four years learning to . . . prance in place? I asked doubtfully.

I suppose the subtle art of the alta escuela *would*

be lost on a cow horse from the provinces, he replied, curling his upper lip.

In reply, I slowed my trot to mimic the step that Campeón had demonstrated. The horse master laughed in surprise. Campeón only snorted and retreated into a silent sulk. Even so, his black-tipped ears swiveled in all directions to take in gossip from every corner of creation.

Presently, the mares were chattering about the taste of different wild flowers, and de Haro was explaining the art of *doma clásica* riding to Rico. The boy was listening politely, but his eyes were glazed. He had spoken little since the journey began.

At first, he had protested when Ana Sofia asked de Haro to take him to Córdoba. But Ana Sofia had a will of iron beneath her honey-sweet voice and silken manners.

"Your brother is suited for the life of a vaquero, but you are cut from different cloth," she told Rico. "Had your father lived, he would have sent you to study at one of the academies in Paris or Milan. Since we have not the silver to spare, apprenticing yourself to Señor de Haro is surely the Lord's way of providing. And how proud I will be to say that I have one son who manages a great hacienda and another who trains horses in the king's court."

So Rico had gone with de Haro and said nothing more about his own wishes. I wondered if he even knew them. He was always so quick to do as he was told.

At the end of the day, our party rested at an inn called the Three Crowns—a grander name than it deserved. Its stable was filled with musty straw, the ceiling so low that cobwebs tickled my ears. De Haro checked our mangers himself to see that we had gotten the ration of corn he had paid for.

Later, Campeón told me that the huge sum of silver de Haro had brought to the horse fair had been stolen from his room at a lodging house in the night. Only by the authority of the Crown had he been able to secure a loan in Seville to make his purchases.

As we traveled, I noticed that our party was greeted with more glares and pleas for charity than smiles and raised sombreros.

There are people who think it wrong for the king to fill his stables with pretty horses when many of his subjects have no bread for their tables, said Campeón.

He was not shy with his opinion that the horse master had paid too much for me. The profit from the king's salt mines, which funded the stables, was not enough to allow for such lavishing of silver, he informed me.

Campeón had opinions on many other subjects as well, and I had no choice but to hear them all. At last we reached Córdoba, a city of pale stone against the lush green of the surrounding forest. We crossed a massive stone bridge over a river and passed through an arched gateway into the city.

The streets were paved with the same ivory-colored rock that formed many of the buildings. It felt cool and slippery underfoot after the hot sand of the country roads.

I leaped into the air as a loud gong sounded above my head. It came from a nearby building with a high tower inlaid with a dizzying pattern of diamonds, checkers, and arches. The noise repeated once, twice, three times. De Haro shortened the reins and closed his legs around my sides to steady me.

No need to shy—it is only the bells of Saint

Vincent, said Campeón, lifting his hooves high so they would clop musically on the cobblestones.

Beyond the noisy building, we entered a market filled with brightly colored tents and carpets. Vendors called out in singsong voices to sell their pottery, cloth, fruit, and spices. Many of the people were dressed like de Haro, in richly colored

silk and velvet. Others wore homespun tunics of sheep's wool. Some of the women wore veils that covered their faces.

Rico was so distracted by the sights that he nearly steered Campeón into a stall brimming with wine jugs. I wished I could have stayed in that market for hours, taking in the sights and

tasting some of the fruits piled temptingly on the woven rugs.

But de Haro pressed me forward, and we continued our march through the city until we reached a stone wall with a wrought-iron gate. De Haro rang a brass bell set in an alcove.

The gate swung open, and I entered a rectangular courtyard lined with shade trees. A fountain in the center bubbled into a round trough of polished marble, topped by a bronze statue of a rearing colt.

A dozen young men in black coats and white breeches appeared from an arched doorway at the far end of the yard. They unhitched the tired carriage horses and led the thirsty mares to water.

De Haro dismounted and handed over my

reins. The saddle was whisked from my back, and my bridle was replaced with a neck collar of buttery soft leather. A silk sheet bearing the king's lion crest was draped across my back.

When the mares had drunk their fill, I pulled my handler forward so that I could slake my own thirst. The water was as fresh and cold as if it had come from a mountain stream.

Campeón splashed his muzzle noisily into the water and remarked that we would finally have a decent meal after the cow fodder we had been served on our journey.

The royal horses eat only the plumpest oats and sweetest corn, toasted with barley syrup and linseed oil to make our coats shine, he prattled. *I do hope my boy, Gabino, will file my hooves tonight—they are chipped to ruin from the stony paths.*

All around me, the courtyard walls were so high that only a square of blue sky was visible above. I craned my neck to look back through the gate, which had shut behind us.

A small brown bird landed on the bronzed colt statue and began singing sweetly. I was suddenly reminded of Ana Sofia's pet nightingale in its golden cage.

A shudder ran through me so that I danced away from my handler and let out a high, ringing whinny to no one at all. In truth, I was more afraid of the walls around me than I had ever been of Joaquin's spurs or the cattle's horns.

Was my beautiful new home a palace or a prison?

8

Desbocado

The royal stables held all the comforts that Campeón had promised—and all the confinement I had feared. The interior was cool and surprisingly bright, with glass skylights that checkered the floor with sunshine. The stables housed more than two hundred horses, with new expansions built every year. Each stone aisle had a double row of straight stalls divided by wooden half walls topped with polished golden bars.

Silken tails swished contentedly on shining haunches. Low whinnies of conversation passed back and forth down the aisle. I was secured in my stall by a short chain to a ring on the wall, within reach of a manger that was always filled with tender timothy hay and twice a day with sweetened grain.

De Haro ran the stables precisely by the cathedral clock tower that struck its chime across the entire city. After breakfast at precisely six each morning, all the horses were groomed until our coats shone like copper, jet, and pearl. Each horse was matched with a rider, and it was always Rico who looked after me, taking his orders from the older boys.

When it was time for lessons, we horses were fitted with small close-cut saddles that allowed us to sense our rider's every movement. To my relief, our bits were simple jointed snaffles that were far milder than the vaqueros' long-shanked curb bits and *serretas*.

The stables had a covered arena, which de Haro had built so his students could train in any weather. Apparently, the royal horses were incapable of working outdoors in the heat or rain.

Each horse and rider trained for three hours each day. Much of that time I spent in the pillars, a pair of matched marble posts. How inoffensive they looked until I spent hours tethered between them, learning to prance until I hated the sight of them!

The goal of this exercise was to produce collection and impulsion, which de Haro regarded
as the two greatest virtues in life. After morning schooling, he commanded Rico to stay and
watch the more advanced students practice the
quadrille, in which four matched pairs of horses
performed a complex pattern in unison.

Campeón assured me that when my work in
the pillars was satisfactory, I would join them. But
to what end? None of the other horses seemed to
question why they were being asked to perform
these endless drills. They were so obedient that
they barely even strained against their lead ropes
if a mare was led by.

Fortunate creatures, the royal broodmares
spent most of their days running free in pasture-
land just outside the city. They were brought in

only for those stallions who had mastered the highest levels of de Haro's silly training.

How I missed the freedom to wander the Moreno orchards as I pleased or gallop free with the cattle and mares on the Andalusian plains! I often became so bored in my stall that I struck my hoof against the stone wall or raked my teeth against the metal bars.

This, at least, had the effect of drowning out the ridiculous conversation of my stablemates.

Campeón, I have been wondering all week and I simply must ask: What does your stableboy do to impart such a wonderful shine to your hooves? I can nearly see my reflection in them.

You are kind to notice, Estrellar. I believe it is a mixture of linseed oil and duck fat.

One day during training, I reached the limits

of my patience. Instead of moving forward with quiet impulsion, I threw my body into reverse and snapped the leather lines that tethered me to the pillars.

But there was nowhere I could run, really, except in endless circles around the arena.

"No horse in this stable has more spirit than Calvino," de Haro said to Rico as the boy led me, sweating and steaming, back to my stall. "I believe he could master any of the airs above the ground. But his spirit is his downfall. If he fails to see the point of an exercise, he explodes like a child having a tantrum. I hesitate to breed from him for fear he will produce foals as unruly as himself."

"He is much like my brother, Joaquin," said Rico with a faint smile. "Perhaps that is why they worked so well together."

"Willfulness may well be a virtue on a cattle ranch, but if Calvino does not soon settle his mind to his work, I may be forced to sell him. I hear there is a shortage of strong young horses for the cavalry, and the king's crusade against the English Protestants shows no signs of ending soon."

Rico looked troubled as he removed my tack and polished it with a muslin cloth. After I had cooled from my unscheduled gallop, he led me out to the courtyard to drink.

There, standing before the fountain, was the most beautiful mare I had ever seen. Her coat was pale, shimmering gold. Her mane and tail were a cream-colored cascade that nearly brushed the ground.

"*Buenos dias,*" said a young girl who was

holding her reins. "I am Isabella de Haro."

"The horse master's daughter?" asked Rico,
staring at the girl. She wore a tightly laced dress
of emerald green, slit up one side for riding. Her

hair was the exact golden shade of her horse, curled elaborately on her head.

"Yes. I have just returned from the villa of my cousin the Duchess of Navarre, where I have spent the summer," she said. The golden mare stepped forward to sniff me in greeting. The damp fur of her muzzle was softer than velvet.

"Your horse is beautiful," said Rico, backing me away after too brief a moment.

"Thank you," said Isabella, her face warming into a smile that made her look like the child she was, under all her finery. "Her name is Mariposa. She was bred here by my father. Are you one of his students?"

"Yes, my name is Enrico Moreno." Rico kept his eyes shyly on the toes of his boots as he spoke.

"Do you ride this stallion?" asked Isabella,

touching my nose with her gloved hand.

Rico nodded. "He was bred on my family's hacienda. Your father bought him at the Seville horse fair this April."

"He's like a unicorn from a fairy tale," said Isabella. "And look—he and Mariposa make a perfect pair. He is silver and she is gold."

Rico and Isabella smiled at each other.

"Speaking of my father, I must tell him I have arrived safely," she said. "Perhaps later we can take our horses for a ride in the garden of the Alcázar of Córdoba, just on the other side of these walls. Have you been there?"

"No," said Rico. "Señor de Haro has kept me busy with my training and lessons."

"My father is a stern taskmaster," said Isabella with a laugh. "You must not take him too seriously if you ever want to have any fun." Then she sighed, the smile fading from her face. "But I envy you," she said.

"Why?" asked Rico in surprise.

"My father will not let me train with his students because I am a girl. And I have to wear layers of petticoats and ride in this stupid side-saddle."

"Is it difficult?" asked Rico, looking curiously at Mariposa's saddle with the jutting leg rest in the middle of the seat.

"Just try training your horse with only one leg to signal him!" Isabella retorted. "How I wish I could sit astride like a boy and not have to go to foolish balls and banquets all the time."

Several days passed before de Haro permitted Rico a free hour to visit the gardens. In that time,

I discovered that Mariposa and Isabella shared a terrible flaw.

They were both smitten with Campeón, champion of trotting between two posts without ever going anywhere. Isabella fussed over "Campie" as if he were a stuffed toy. She plied him with sugar and braided matching flowers into his and Mariposa's manes. Worst of all, Mariposa didn't even seem to mind. Her teardrop nostrils quivered with affection whenever she saw the fat prancer.

Otherwise, Mariposa was perfect in every way. Rico seemed surprised by my unusual gentleness and obedience as the four of us strolled through the garden that lay like a hidden jewel in the center of Córdoba, with a great stone castle at its heart.

"The Alcázar is where the king stays when he visits the city," Isabella explained to Rico. "It was built by the Moors when they ruled over Spain—my father says they were the greatest architects in the world, and even their fortresses were built with magnificent gardens surrounding them. Unless the king is here, they are open to the public so that all can appreciate their beauty."

The paths were paved with glittering chips of white quartz, and they surrounded beds of exotic flowers, blossoming mulberry trees, and rectangular pools with fountains that sent many crossing jets of water into the air.

I have never seen a horse of your exquisite coloring before, I remarked to Mariposa as she reached down to snuffle the iridescent feathers of a peacock that had wandered onto the path.

Mares of my pale shade were favored by Queen Isabella of Castile, she replied. *Thus, horses like me came to be known as Golden Isabellas. The horse master gave me as a gift to his own Isabella for that reason.*

We passed through a grove of orange trees. I lifted my head to sniff their sweet, familiar scent. I told Mariposa of my life on the hacienda, from my foalhood encounter with the lynx to my work with the cattle on the range.

Our riders drew us to a halt to allow a cart filled with elegantly dressed ladies to pass. Suddenly, I realized that I was outside the locked stable gates for the first time since I had come to Córdoba.

If I were to bolt and lose my rider, I might reach the bridge leading out of the city. From there, instinct would lead me back to the Moreno estate. Or perhaps I could go straight to the mountains and form my own band of wild mares.

In any case, would it not be better to chase freedom than stay trapped in my golden cage? Mariposa seemed to sense my thoughts. She looked steadily at me with her dark almond eye.

Campeón has told me that the horse master may sell you to the general of the cavalry if you continue to resist his training, she said. *But you are far too fine to end up in a muddy battlefield, and I would be sorry to lose your company.*

In that moment, I resolved to do nothing that might cause us to be parted. And if Campeón set the bar for her affections, I would master any form of prancing necessary to leave him in my dust.

9

A Dance of Hearts

For the next two years, that is exactly what I did. I learned how to move correctly in each gait and how to shorten and lengthen my stride at the walk, trot, and canter. Next came lateral work, in which I learned to change the bend of my neck and body. Many of the movements were familiar because I had performed them naturally while working with the cattle. But now they had become an art form in themselves.

Rico was no longer the shy, uncertain boy who had turned the other cheek to his brother's mocking. Now it seemed he spoke little because he could say much with few words. His signals to me were slight because they were perfectly clear. He held up his head in a way that seemed to say he had finally found his place in the world.

I suppose that I had found my place as well. I had been as docile as a child's hobbyhorse for months—for Mariposa's sake—and de Haro had allowed me to join the quadrille. There was something satisfying in working so closely with the other stallions, learning to sense their most subtle moods and movements. But it seemed a cruel twist of fate that I was partnered with Campeón and forced to mirror his dainty strides.

Isabella and Mariposa spent about half their time in Córdoba and half visiting relatives in Spain and France. Our many rides in the garden of the Alcázar were a welcome break from de Haro's rigid schedule.

But my life was not all work—there were games as well. Sometimes the students played *sortija*, trying to spear a lance through a ring suspended by a cord while the horses galloped at full speed. Other times we played *carosello*, our riders tossing a clay ball between them. I discovered the consequences of losing when Rico dropped the ball and it smashed at my feet. My legs and belly were doused with rose-scented perfume.

"You and Calvino will smell as pretty as a

princess for days!" gloated Gabino, who had thrown the ball. I noticed that Campeón often appeared to shy when Gabino was in midcatch— I think he enjoyed smelling like a rose.

Of all de Haro's students, Rico seemed to take his training the most seriously. One evening, he spent what seemed like hours schooling me on a single movement, the cantering half pass. If done correctly, I would move smoothly along a diagonal line, my legs crossing each other while my head and body stayed facing to the front.

It was a difficult movement even in the trot. It was exhausting in the canter. Repeated endlessly, it was torturous. I ground my teeth on the bit as Rico turned me down the quarter line for the thousandth time.

Just then, Mariposa and Isabella entered the

arena. Mariposa whinnied to me, and I took the opportunity to divert my course and greet her properly.

"There is flamenco music in the garden this evening," said Isabella, watching while Rico made me back half the length of the arena in reprimand. "Won't you come see it with me? I do so love to dance."

I could hear strains of music muffled by the thick stable walls. How I wished I were there instead of here!

Rico sighed. "I cannot. I promised your father I would work with Calvino until our half pass was perfection itself. But it is not even halfway to perfection."

"Well, if you will not dance with me, perhaps Calvino will dance with Mariposa."

They trotted in a collected circle around us. Although Isabella complained about having to ride sidesaddle, she was nearly as skilled as Rico. Mariposa fairly floated across the ground.

Without waiting for my rider's permission, I sprang forward and fell into step beside Mariposa. Rico held his arms stiffly for a moment, then relented. Mariposa and I trotted around the ring with perfectly matched strides. How much nicer it was than being paired with Campeón!

Then Mariposa and Isabella broke away and halted, facing us from across the arena. Rico rode me forward at the Spanish walk, my legs raised high and extended straight in front of me. Isabella backed Mariposa away while I moved toward her.

At the edge of the arena, we reversed. Now Mariposa stepped forward with flashing legs while

I backed up, my hind legs tucked under me and my neck curved like a tightly drawn bow. Then we did a half turn on the haunches together and sprang forward into a canter.

I was farther from Mariposa than I wanted to be, so I stepped over in a perfect half pass. When I had reached Mariposa's side, it seemed the most natural thing in the world for Rico to reach out and take Isabella's hand. They pirouetted around each other as if they were twirling in a waltz.

I heard a cough from the doorway. The horse master was standing there with his arms crossed in front of his chest.

"So this is what you call training?" he asked dryly.

"Don't be angry, Father," said Isabella as Rico quickly let go of her hand and returned to his schooling exercises. "Rico was practicing your silly drills like a perfect tin soldier until Mariposa and I distracted him."

"I am not angry, for you have given me an

idea," said de Haro, pacing thoughtfully. Even the dust from the sandy arena dared not cling to his perfectly polished boots.

"King Philip will be arriving to tour the royal stables next month," de Haro continued. "His Majesty has requested me to create a demonstration to impress the diplomats who are traveling with him."

"The king himself at the stables, how exciting!" cried Isabella.

"Indeed," said de Haro with less enthusiasm. "I believe the quadrille shows the precision of my training methods. But the nobles today are spoiled by culture. They expect poetry as well as perfection. The two of you—and I will speak with you later, Rico—have given me an idea. I will offer the king a ballet on horseback, set to music."

De Haro's hands moved as he spoke, painting in the air a picture of his imagined performance. I would never have guessed the horse master to have such a romantic nature.

Soon he was directing Isabella as if she were one of the riders in his academy, and she couldn't have looked more pleased. At last she was a student in the royal stables, even if she still had to ride sidesaddle.

Our exhibit was held in the spacious outdoor arena. A silk tent shielded the king and his party from the sun, and a violin player entertained them while they waited. The noblemen and their wives reminded me of the peacocks in the garden of the Alcázar.

However, King Philip wore a simple black tunic with a white ruffled collar. His pale gray eyes held the intensity of a wolf observing a herd of fallow deer.

He sat in silence while we performed the quadrille with clockwork perfection. I set aside my dislike of Campeón for the occasion and did not even lay back my ears when we passed on the diagonal. Finally, the eight horses came to a square halt and our riders removed their hats in salute.

The king and his company clapped politely, but they did not seem moved. I noticed de Haro frowning at the cool reception.

I remained in the ring while the other horses

filed out, and de Haro announced a special performance, *el baile de corazones*—the dance of hearts.

Mariposa and Isabella entered the arena. Isabella wore a scarlet dress and carried an embroidered fan. Mariposa wore matching scarlet ribbons in her mane and tail.

The violinist began to play again. I danced for Mariposa with all the expressiveness I could muster, and she for me. Isabella fluttered her fan and Rico held his arm outstretched until at last they joined hands in a cantering pirouette.

At the end of our performance, I halted before Mariposa and lowered myself onto one knee with the other leg stretched out before me. Rico and I had been practicing our final bow in secret for weeks.

The applause was louder and longer this time. I saw de Haro speaking with the king as Rico led me past the silk tent for a well-earned rest.

The next day, Isabella ran into the stable while Rico was grooming me. "I have just returned from a masquerade ball for the royal diplomats," she said in a rush. "There was so much gossip, my ears were burning. Everyone loved our performance except the Dutch ambassador. He called the king's stallions 'parade horses.' He said they would look more at home in the ballet than on the battlefield."

Rico laughed, and Isabella made a wry face. "You have seen the king—he is cold as marble," she said. "But the color rose in his pale cheeks and he stood up from his seat at the table. He said he would test the Spanish horse in games of war against the mounts of any other nation. By the time dinner was over, it had been settled. There is going to be a bullfight!"

Rico gasped. "But the corrida was banned by the pope," he said. "My family's cattle were only ever tested as yearlings, never as grown bulls, as they were in my grandfather's time."

"The king was so angered by the Dutch ambassador that he called for the pope to reverse the decree," said Isabella. "The fight will take place at El Escorial, the king's palace in Madrid."

Isabella paused, and her face grew somber. "The king has already chosen which of his horses will represent the Crown," she said. "One will be my father's beloved Campeón—and the other will be Calvino."

10

Games of War

The king was not a man of wasted words. Within a fortnight, Campeón and I had been moved to the stables at Madrid. The palace of El Escorial, set apart from the city, was stark and a bit gloomy compared to lively, decorative Córdoba.

But we were not here for the scenery. From

dawn until dusk, the horse master drilled Rico and Gabino in mounted combat. For the first time, Campeón and I faced off as if in battle instead of working together in harmony.

My life as a ranch horse had made me fast and strong, but all that prancing between the pillars had taught me to keep my balance centered, ready for sudden movement in any direction. The slightest shift in Rico's weight could signal his strategy while revealing nothing to the enemy.

In Córdoba, I would have relished these games of war. But now I felt that Campeón and I were united against an uncertain fate. When he continued to leave his flank unguarded, I attacked it mercilessly—not to best him, but to prepare us for a more fearsome enemy.

Between Campeón's disdain of the "inferior"

oats and our relentless training, the bay stallion's plumpness melted away. I hoped the perfection of his form would be enough to save him. The horse master's pet had never faced another creature with a killing gleam in its eye. His snorting and stamping had an element of show, as if we were practicing for another piece of royal theater.

On the day of the corrida, Rico dressed in a traditional vaquero outfit like the one his brother had worn to the horse fair. For his shirtwaist, Rico wore the silk handkerchief Isabella had given him during our last ride through the garden of the Alcázar.

The horse master's daughter had begged to come with us, but her father would not allow it. I had savored my last moments with Mariposa, trying to remember the curve of her neck and her exact shade of gold, in case I never saw her again.

Rico and Gabino rode us through the crowd that had gathered on the palace grounds. The high walls of the arena the king had built were draped with multicolored banners. Musicians and clowns entertained the spectators.

The royal balcony was set high above the arena. King Philip was dressed in black again, although he had added a scarlet cape to his outfit, and he wore the royal crown upon his head. Queen Anna sat beside him, engulfed in a vast purple gown of many layers, and the young prince sat on her lap.

Beside me, Campeón was fretting because Gabino had forgotten to shine his hooves. *I just don't feel right without it,* he complained, prancing in an anxious *piaffe.* We reached a corded-off area

near the arena gates, and I had my first glimpse of the other horses who had been caught up in this contest of pride.

The Dutch ambassador had sent a single, gleaming black Friesian, claiming the horse was unequaled in all the world. England had chosen a destrier of even greater size and a sleek bay courser. France sent a pair of cream-colored trotters from the royal stables of the House of Valois, and Naples picked two sturdy horses from its cavalry. A lone Barb, as delicate as a yearling and with a dished face, represented Spain's former rulers, the Moors.

Each horse and rider wore the tack and clothing of his own country. But we would all enter the corrida with the same weapons, bound by the same rules.

We would all be matched against a *toro bravo*, a "brave bull" bred especially for his fierceness. The winners would be the horse and rider who preserved themselves from injury, made a clean kill, and entertained the audience with the most daring show.

Our first weapon would be the banderillas, two poles with sharp spikes at the end. These would be stuck into the bull's neck to weaken his muscles. Second was a pair of flower-shaped rosettes with spiky points to be pinned into the bull's neck from close range. Finally, each rider would attempt to kill the bull with a single sword strike to the heart.

The riders drew lots to determine our order. Rico and I would fight last.

First to enter the arena was the destrier from

England. The slow-moving warhorse, decorated with colorful textiles and glinting armored plates, was like a painted target for the *toro bravo*. The bull mauled him badly and dragged his rider from the saddle. Only his knight's steel armor saved him from being crushed to death. A pair of toreros jumped into the arena, waving scarlet capes to distract the bull.

The bay courser was quicker but possessed too little courage—or too much wisdom—to let his rider get close enough to place the banderillas.

The first cream-colored trotter had his turn. The bull's opening charge made him senseless with fear, so that he bolted to the arena's edge and leaped wildly into the crowd.

Next came the Dutch ambassador's Friesian. The black horse and the black bull made a striking pair in the ring. The stallion was agile for his size, and brave. His rider struck the bull with all the banderillas and rosettes. The crowd began to cheer.

But the Friesian's rider faltered in the final blow. His sword lodged in the thick muscle of the bull's neck but did not pierce deep enough to kill. Like all the other contestants, his bull was slain by one of the toreros' blades.

Like all the others, he had failed.

Campeón was next to enter the arena. De Haro's training had made him quick and strong. His eyes were white-rimmed with anxiety, but he remained obedient to Gabino. The boy managed to stick both banderillas and one of the rosettes into the shoulder of his small but unusually vicious rust-colored bull.

Then Campeón fell into an old error and left his flank unguarded. When Gabino drew alongside the bull to drive the sword into his heart, the animal gouged his horns deep into Campeón's haunches. The toreros drew the bull's attention, and Gabino rode Campeón, limping, from the ring.

For the first time that day, I felt fear rising in my heart. I pawed nervously and pulled at the reins. Rico stroked my neck, but his hand felt clammy and cold. Neither of us was comforted when the second cream-colored trotter and then the first horse from Naples emerged from the corrida with deep wounds and battered riders.

Last before me came the Barb, a chestnut with a white blaze running like a streak of lightning down his face. And he moved as if lightning had entered his body. The bull's horns never grazed his sides, and the Moor was the first to slay his *toro bravo*. The crowd cheered long and loud for him.

Rico and I were the last pair remaining. I entered the arena at my loftiest canter and halted in front of the Imperial balcony. Rico asked me to bow as I had done for Mariposa and Isabella.

I knelt before the king, then reared up into a *pesade*. The crowd murmured with appreciation. I wondered if the Dutch ambassador was making another comment about Spain's parade horses.

A trumpet sounded. The toreros opened the gate beneath King Philip's balcony and released my opponent into the arena.

The Hour of Truth

The bull was the largest of his kind I had seen. His muscles rippled beneath a coat like polished coal as he trotted into the arena on surprisingly delicate hooves.

The blur of the crowd, the blare of trumpets, and the motion of the toreros and their capes fell away. There was only me, my rider, and the *toro bravo*.

He grew still as a statue when he saw me. His glittering black eyes held a calculating look. I stepped forward in a lofty Spanish walk and halted about ten paces in front of him. The bull lowered his head and scraped the ground with one cloven hoof.

I tossed my head, laid back my ears, and snapped my teeth in the air. The bull took a few threatening steps forward, shaking his horns. I backed up, maintaining the distance between us. The bull broke into a trot. I continued to face him, my legs trembling with the effort of traveling so quickly in reverse.

The bull dug his hooves into the deep sand and charged. At the last possible moment, I

arced my body sideways so that the horns struck only air.

Three more times, Rico circled me back to approach the bull. Each time, he held me in check until the sharp horns nearly brushed my flanks. Then he released the reins and let me sprint away. My powerful hindquarters and fluttering tail served the same taunting purpose as the toreros' capes.

Finally, Rico drew up to the arena's edge to collect the first of the sharpened banderillas. The contest was a deadly dance for both me and my opponent now.

I cantered diagonally in front of the bull so our bodies formed a *T*. The move was identical to the half pass that Rico and I had practiced at Córdoba, but with far more at stake if I faltered.

At last I truly understood the horse master's endless drills on collection and impulsion—they were the means by which I was now evading death.

Rico drew me in ever-tighter circles around my opponent. Then, quick as a snake strike, he reached his right arm across his body and stuck the banderilla into the bull's neck.

The animal snorted as if flames would shoot

out of his nostrils instead of air, and he chased me at a blind gallop. Anger had made him lose caution, and Rico leaned down to place the second banderilla as I sidestepped the charge.

The bull skidded to a stiff-legged halt. Blood flowed freely down his neck, and his head hung low. I sensed reluctance in my rider as he rode me over to collect the flower-shaped rosettes. Nonetheless, we gave the audience the death-defying spectacle they wished to see.

I galloped with my body angled sideways, showing my belly, taunting the bull by staying just beyond the reach of those wickedly curving horns.

Then Rico asked me to pirouette. Here, of all places?

But I made one, two, three, fast circles in front

of the bull, still cantering forward even as I spun. The audience roared with approval.

Rico dropped the reins onto my neck and held up the rosettes, one in each hand. Using only his legs to guide me, Rico spun me back to face the bull. I curved my body around the animal's horns as it charged again. At just the right moment, Rico leaned down and pinned both rosettes.

By now, the bull was panting from the heat and his injuries. Rico rode me over to where the horse master stood at the arena's edge, holding the sword for his student.

"Must I kill him, Diego?" asked Rico urgently. "I have heard that in Portugal, they only thrust the sword into the air as a symbol of victory, and the animal's life is spared."

"The bull is already gravely injured," said

de Haro. "But I believe your skill will let you succeed where others have failed, and make this animal's death a quick and honorable one."

Rico took the sword and held it at arm's length with the point facing the sky. The audience was silent now, for the hour of truth had arrived.

It was over in only moments. The bull saw the glint of the sword, and we fell into our now familiar game of advance and retreat. Then Rico asked me to double back behind the bull so that I cantered beside him. Recalling Campeón's mistake, I kept close to the animal's side so that he had no room to turn and gore me.

Rico raised the sword high and drove it deep between the bull's shoulders. Then he drew me to a halt and dismounted to face the dying animal on foot, as courageous *rejoneadors* did.

The bull had weakened fast, but he was not defeated yet. He lunged forward in a final attack. Rico leaped back, but he would not have been quick enough if I hadn't sunk my teeth into the nape of the bull's neck.

The sharp horns raked my foreleg, but I held fast. Our blood mixed together on the ground. The crowd's cheers thundered in my ears and became indistinguishable from the pounding of my heart.

The bull's knees buckled. Rico grabbed me by the reins and backed me out of the life-and-death embrace. Then he touched his hand to his lips and pressed his palm against the bull's forehead in a final gesture of respect.

The animal fell to his side and lay still. His eyes were closed; his battle was over.

Applause crashed over us like breaking waves. Rico raised his arms high, then bowed low. His face was somber, mirroring none of the crowd's glee.

"Will you not take the ears as a trophy?" called one of the toreros as Rico mounted and rode me toward the arena gates.

"My horse has been injured," said Rico. "I must see to him."

I shied as we passed the bull's body. It was the nature of the animal to fight, but in the wild a defeated rival could retreat. This creature's fate had been sealed from the moment he entered the arena.

But even though the contest was not a fair one, we had fought as equals in courage, and he had earned the name of *toro bravo*.

12

A Horse of Kings

De Haro found Rico in my stall. The gash on my leg had not cut into the tendon or bone. It hardly hurt now that it was washed and bandaged and I had a pail of oats to occupy me.

"Don't you wish to feast at the palace?"

de Haro asked Rico as the boy sat in the straw beside my manger. "Everyone has gathered in your honor. Even the Dutch ambassador wants to ride home on a Spanish horse."

"I fear my appetite is spoiled by my conscience," murmured Rico. He watched me digging in to my supper. "I envy horses, who live in the moment and have no troubled dreams."

"You know I dislike the blood sport of the corrida," said de Haro. "I like to believe it is not what I have trained my horses for. But the truth is that *doma clásica* developed to make Spain victorious in war. Today, you proved its value to those who dismissed it as frivolous. You have made me proud."

Rico looked up at de Haro. I knew the horse

master was the one man whose approval could take the place of what Rico could never receive from his father.

De Haro cleared his throat. "The king was so pleased with Calvino that he wishes to keep him as his royal mount," he said gently. "He will ride him in the Corpus Christi parade before all the citizens of Madrid and keep him here at El Escorial."

A war of emotions played on Rico's face, pride fighting with sorrow.

Sensing his distress, I left my oats and went over to him. I pressed my head to his chest while he rubbed my neck under my heavy mane.

"You have learned all that I can teach you of horsemanship," de Haro said to Rico. "If you are willing, I would send you to the Neapolitan riding

academy to study with Grisone and Pignatelli."

So little Rico—no longer very little, at fifteen—went to Italy to ride with the greatest horsemen in the world. And I remained in Madrid with the king.

On the day of the Corpus Christi parade, plates of armor were placed on my head, neck, and back. Scarlet tapestries bearing the king's crest hung from my saddle and reins. The king wore a suit of polished parade armor, so heavy that it took two men to help him into my saddle.

We led the procession through the streets. Red-and-gold banners and wreaths of evergreen hung from balconies. The ground was scattered with fragrant rosemary and thyme, and people threw flowers in our path.

Behind the king, four priests carried a golden

chalice under a silk canopy. A choir of children dressed like angels followed, chanting hymns. The people of the city raised their voices with them.

On this day they forgot whether they were rich or poor, merchant or peasant. They were all glad to be Spanish, joined in celebration of their Lord and their king. I stepped high and proud, with my tail flowing like a silver banner behind me.

After the parade, the king lingered in the stable to speak with the horse master about his breeding project. He had replaced his armor with a simple woolen tunic and could have been mistaken for a scribe or a schoolteacher.

"I believe I have shown once and for all the superiority of my 'parade horses,'" the king said to de Haro, a smile flitting across his thin face.

"Truly, the kindness of the breed is the greatest thing His Majesty possesses," the horse master replied. "I believe it exceeds even their courage."

King Philip granted de Haro a generous measure of silver to expand the stables and buy enough land for 1,200 horses.

Nearly every afternoon, the king took me hunting with his falcon in the primeval woods of El Escorial. We rode in parades throughout the cities of his empire, from the towering castles and cathedrals of Vienna to the whitewashed cottages and turquoise waters of Gibraltar.

When three years had passed, the king grew anxious to see my foals and sent me back to Córdoba.

Mariposa was there, as golden as my memories.

Her filly was my first to be born, a dapple gray with fluttering nostrils that reminded me of Rasula.

Rico had become a celebrated rider at the academy in Naples. He lived there with Isabella, whom he had married. When they visited Córdoba, the four of us always took an evening ride in the garden of the Alcázar.

Another old friend was at the stables, too. His battle scar had made him something of a hero, and a limp kept him from rejoining the quadrille. So Campeón told the tale of his bravery in the corrida to anyone who would listen, had his hooves polished daily, and sired many plump foals with a talent for prancing.

My own colts and fillies multiplied to fill the royal studbook. They were sent as wedding gifts to distant kings. They secured alliances and soothed hostilities between nations. They crossed the ocean in vast ships to a land that no horses had seen in my lifetime.

Sculptors cast the image of my foals in marble and bronze. Painters captured their likenesses on canvas. Several of my grandfoals were sent to Austria, where a new academy for *alta escuela* was being formed.

As for Spain, she flourished, too. Another king bearing Philip's name succeeded him, and he also prized beautiful horses. The fields surrounding Córdoba were filled with mares and foals, many of them dapple-gray like the first mares brought from Andalusia.

Visitors to Spain came to see the royal stables. They admired the decorative buildings and the regal stallions. They heard the music of the country. They drank her wine and ate her juicy oranges and fragrant olives. They watched her savage sports.

And they wondered: How did this land between two continents, in love with tradition and divided by war, come to rule an empire so vast that the sun never set on its rule?

I do not know for certain, but some have said it is because the Spanish horses are the finest in the world.

APPENDIX

ALL THE KING'S HORSES

The name Philip means "lover of horses" in ancient Greek. It was a fitting choice for King Philip II, son of the Holy Roman Emperor Charles V. Philip II inherited the rule of Spain and Portugal and was also the king of England and Ireland during his marriage to Queen Mary I.

The king was a devout Catholic and often waged war against the English Protestants. His territory included colonies on every settled continent, as far away as the Philippine Islands in Southeast Asia.

The king was also a skillful equestrian. In 1567, he ordered his horse master, a nobleman named Diego López de Haro, to buy 1,200 of the best horses in the provinces and create a new, highly refined breed. Many of these horses came from Andalusia.

The royal horses of Córdoba became renowned across the world. They were impossible for ordinary people to buy at any price. Famous artists such as Diego Velázquez and El Greco painted portraits of royalty mounted on beautiful Spanish horses.

By the late 1700s, leggy Thoroughbreds from England had become the fashionable mounts of the nobility. Many Spanish horses died of plague and famine in the eighteenth century, and the original stables at Córdoba were destroyed by a fire in 1734. Today, they have been rebuilt as a UNESCO World Heritage Site. People can tour the barns and see equestrian performances like those that once entertained kings and queens.

DOMA VAQUERA AND *DOMA CLÁSICA*

The *doma vaquera* style of riding was developed by Spanish ranchers whose survival depended on the agility and courage of their mounts. Like Western riders in the United States, Spanish vaqueros ride with one hand on the reins, keeping the other free to hold a *garrocha* pole.

Doma vaquera is also a judged sport in which riders show off their horses' paces in a series of figures at the walk and canter. The patterns also include pirouettes, rein backs, side passes, and other moves that horses might use to work with the unpredictable Andalusian cattle.

While *doma vaquera* riding began on the Andalusian plains, *doma clásica* riding developed on Europe's battlefields. The first riding school was opened in 1532 in Naples, which was then a part of the Spanish empire. Its founder, Federico Grisone, claimed to be inspired by the great general Xenophon of ancient Greece.

But unlike Xenophon, who had emphasized

gentleness and harmony, Grisone employed many harsh training methods. The goal of *doma clásica* training was to produce horses with strong forward movement, quick response to signals, and absolute obedience—the ideal mount for war.

In the eighteenth century, horses were replaced by heavy artillery in war. *Doma clásica* became a more stylized form of riding, the foundation of modern dressage. Today, the Royal Andalusian School of Equestrian Art in Jerez hosts *doma clásica* performances for the public.

An Andalusian stallion named Pluto was one of six foundation sires for the Lippizaner breed, which developed at the Spanish Riding School in Vienna. By the late 1700s, these "dancing horses" had become famous around the world.

THE CORRIDA

The bullfight, or corrida, has been part of Spanish culture for more than a thousand years. The first official bullfight took place in 1133 to celebrate the crowning of King Alfonso VIII. However, bulls were used in battle and military training since the time of the Roman Empire.

In the most common form of bullfighting, picadors mounted on armored horses enter the arena first and weaken the bull's neck with sharp lances. A sword-wielding matador then moves in on foot to face the animal alone.

In the older *rejoneador* style, the torero stays mounted for nearly the entire fight, although he may change horses at different phases. The most skilled *rejoneadors* appear to effortlessly outwit the bull while spending much of the fight within inches of its horns. Most bullfights are not officially judged, but the audience will cast a popular vote, cheering for their favorite toreros and heckling those who lack skill.

Bullfighting was banned by Pope Pius V in 1567, but King Philip II reversed the decree. The king was known to dislike bullfighting, but he also acknowledged its importance to the Spanish people.

Today, animal rights groups argue that bullfighting is cruel to the animals, which do not have a choice about whether to participate. Defenders argue that the deaths of fighting bulls are more humane than those of cattle raised for meat. Some people believe the corrida is an essential part of Spanish culture, or even a form of art.

Bullfighting is now illegal in some Spanish

provinces but is allowed in others. The sport continues to be as controversial as it was in King Philip II's time.

THE ANDALUSIAN LEGACY

In Spain, the Andalusian horse is known as the *Pura Raza Española* (PRE). About 80 percent of PREs or Andalusians are gray, with bay and black being the next most common colors. Andalusians typically stand from 15 to 16.2 hands.

The breed standard calls for high, elastic strides; rounded muscular hindquarters; an arched neck; a straight or slightly convex face; and a thick, flowing mane and tail. This type is often called the "baroque" horse. The Andalusian's

temperament should be docile, honest, brave, and quick to learn.

Andalusians were not exported from Spain until 1962. They are still fairly rare in the United States, with about 8,500 registered. The breed's flashy looks and trainability make it a natural choice for circuses, liberty acts, and Hollywood productions. In the *Lord of the Rings* movies, Gandalf's magical horse, Shadowfax, was played by a pair of Andalusian stallions named Domero and Blanco.

ABOUT THE AUTHOR

Whitney Sanderson has loved horses since she was a child, riding in a 4-H club and reading series like The Saddle Club and The Black Stallion. In addition to always having a horse or two in the backyard, she grew up surrounded by beautiful equine artwork created by her mother, Horse Diaries illustrator Ruth Sanderson. Whitney is the author of Horse Diaries #5: *Golden Sun* and Horse Diaries #10: *Darcy*, as well as another chapter book called *Horse Rescue: Treasure*.

ABOUT THE ILLUSTRATOR

Ruth Sanderson grew up with a love for horses. She has illustrated and retold many fairy tales and likes to feature horses in them whenever possible. Her book about a magical horse, *The Golden Mare, the Firebird, and the Magic Ring,* won the Texas Bluebonnet Award.

Ruth and her daughter have two horses, an Appaloosa named Thor and a quarter horse named Gabriel. She lives with her family in Massachusetts.

To find out more about her adventures with horses and the research she does to create Horse Diaries illustrations, visit her website, ruthsanderson.com.

～ Collect all the books in the ～
Horse Diaries series!

HORSE DIARIES

Elska

CATHERINE HAPKA
Illustrated by RUTH SANDERSON

HORSE DIARIES

Bell's Star

ALISON HART
Illustrated by RUTH SANDERSON

HORSE DIARIES

Koda

PATRICIA HERMES
Illustrated by RUTH SANDERSON

HORSE DIARIES

Darcy

WHITNEY SANDERSON
Illustrated by RUTH SANDERSON

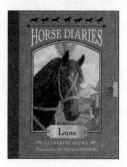

HORSE DIARIES

Luna

CATHERINE HAPKA
Illustrated by RUTH SANDERSON

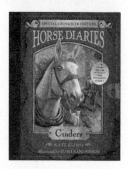

SPECIAL CROSSOVER EDITION

HORSE DIARIES

Cinders

KATE KLIMO
Illustrated by RUTH SANDERSON